13 TERRIFYING SHORT STORIES FOR HALLOWEEN

**13 Terrifying Short Stories for Halloween,
1st Edition**

Story concept, text, and compilation by © 2024 Leanne Staback, Ph.D.

Editing, print preparation, formatting, back cover summary, cover and interior design provided by Staback Author Services.

Books may be ordered through popular, online retailers, the publisher's online store, IngramSpark, or by contacting the publisher at:

Page Turner Books, Inc.®
170 S. Green Valley Pkwy., Suite 300
Henderson, NV 89012-3145

Visit our website at www.ptbooksinc.com or contact us via email at
contact@ptbooksinc.com.

Page Turner Books, Inc.® name and imprint are the trademark and copyright of Page Turner Books, Inc.®

Hardcover ISBN: 978-1-958487-98-3
Paperback ISBN: 978-1-965788-04-2
iBooks ISBN: 978-1-965788-00-4

Printed in the United States of America.

First printing: September 2024.

ATTENTION CORPORATIONS AND ORGANIZATIONS!
Most Page Turner Books, Inc.® publications are available at quantity discounts with bulk purchase for educational, business, or sales promotional use. For information, please visit www.ptbooksinc.com or http://ingramspark.com

13 TERRIFYING SHORT STORIES FOR HALLOWEEN

LEANNE STABACK

PAGE TURNER BOOKS INC.

HENDERSON, NEVADA
UNITED STATES OF AMERICA

TABLE OF CONTENTS

THE SINISTER JACK-O'-LANTERN

Once upon a time, in the small village of Hollow Haven, there stood a haunted house at the edge of the woods. Within the broken-down house, a creepy garden grew, filled with twisted trees and eerie, overgrown plants. But the most chilling presence of all was a gigantic jack-o'-lantern that sat at the center.

Legend had it that this jack-o'-lantern possessed a wicked soul and would come to life on the night of Halloween, seeking to devour any children who dared to approach. All of the children in the village had heard the tales and were warned to stay away from the property.

One night, three friends were talking about the stories they heard about the house, and their curiosity got the better of them. They decided to investigate the haunted garden, doubtful of the danger awaiting them.

As the moon rose high in the sky, casting an eerie glow, these brave children gathered before the house. Amy, Bennett, and Claudia exchanged nervous glances, but their determination pushed them forward.

"We should turn back," whispered Bennett, his voice trembling at the thought that the stories might be more than just stories.

"*No*, we came this far," declared Amy foolishly, trying to sound braver than she felt. "We have to see if the stories are true."

The children tiptoed through the overgrown garden, their hearts pounding in their chests.

When they reached the jack-o'-lantern, its eyes suddenly flickered to life, glowing with an intense, fiery orange light. Its jagged mouth twisted into a sinister grin, revealing sharp, jagged teeth.

"Who dares to enter my garden?" bellowed the jack-o'-lantern, its voice echoing through the night.

The children froze in terror, their eyes wide with fear. The jack-o'-lantern had awakened, and now it hungered for their flesh.

"Well, well, well, what do we have here?" sneered the jack-o'-lantern. "Little morsels who dare to challenge me?"

Amy stepped forward, her voice trembling. "We didn't mean to disturb you. We were just curious."

The jack-o'-lantern let out a wicked laugh. "Curiosity killed the cat, little one. And tonight, it will be your downfall."

"But why do you want to eat us?" asked Claudia, her voice quivering.

The jack-o'-lantern's eyes narrowed, its fiery gaze fixed on the trembling child. "Because it's what I do. I am the embodiment of Halloween's darkness, a creature born to feast on the souls of children."

Bennett mustered his courage and spoke up. "But Halloween is about fun and treats, not terror and evil."

The jack-o'-lantern paused, its fiery eyes flickering with a hint of confusion. "Fun and treats? Is that what Halloween means to you?"

"Yes," Amy interjected. "It's a time for costumes, laughter, and candy. It's not about hurting others."

The jack-o'-lantern's expression softened briefly, a flicker of doubt crossing its twisted features.

"Hmmm...I never considered that."

Claudia took a step forward, her voice filled with empathy.

"Maybe it's time to let go of that darkness. Halloween can be a time for everyone to enjoy, including you."

The jack-o'-lantern's fiery glow dimmed, its menacing aura dissipating.

"You may be right. I've been consumed by my own hunger for far too long."

The children approached the jack-o'-lantern cautiously, their fear replaced with compassion. They reached out and touched its rough, pumpkin skin, offering comfort.

The jack-o-lantern, irritated by their human touch, growled and bit off Claudia's arm as soon as it got close to its mouth.

"Aagh!" Claudia screamed.

Amy and Bennett also screamed as blood spurted from the stump left hanging from Claudia's shoulder. They quickly grabbed Claudia around the waist and wrenched her away from the jack-o-lantern and dragged her out of the haunted garden to safety.

"We have to get her some help fast!" Amy exclaimed.

"I'm calling 9-1-1 right now," Bennett explained frantically as he held his cell phone up to his ear.

They heard the jack-o-lantern laughing from inside the house, and heard it say, "That's what you get for thinking you could pull one over on me!"

Amy and Bennett felt another chill wash over them as they waited for the 9-1-1 operator to pick up.

The operator picked up the call. "9-1-1 what is your emergency?"

"My friend just had her arm bitten off and she's bleeding a lot!" Bennett yelled into the phone.

"Are you in a safe location?" the operator asked.

"I think so," Bennett replied.

"Do you have anything you can tie around her arm to slow the bleeding?"

Amy and Bennett looked around, not seeing anything useful.

"No," Bennett replied morosely.

"Claudia!" Amy said urgently. "Claudia! Wake up!"

Bennett looked at Claudia and was alarmed to see her skin fading to white and her lips turning blue. Claudia appeared to be sleeping, but Bennett knew this wasn't the case.

"I'm sending an ambulance. What is your address?" The operator asked.

Amy and Bennett looked at each other in a panic, not knowing what to say.

"We're in front of a haunted house," Bennett explained to the operator. "I don't see an address!"

"Okay, stay right where you are," the operator instructed. "We can track you...just don't leave that spot until the ambulance gets there."

"Okay," Bennett agreed.

Within minutes they heard the siren of the approaching ambulance, and both children breathed a sigh of relief.

The ambulance stopped at the curb right next to them, and the paramedics quickly exited the vehicle and ran over to Claudia. Bennett and Amy watched as they wrapped a tourniquet around the upper part of Claudia's arm and began taking her vital signs.

Too quickly, the paramedics stopped and sat back on their heels.

"She's gone," the lead paramedic said quietly.

"Gone?!" Amy yelled. "What do you mean?"

"She's gone," he explained. "She's dead. She bled to death."

"NO!" Bennett yelled and began crying. "You're wrong! She's NOT dead! She can't be..."

"I'm sorry," a female paramedic said and placed her arm gently on Bennett's shoulder.

"How did this happen?" A police officer who had just arrived asked.

Amy explained about the pumpkin and how it attacked Claudia when she touched it, and how it all happened so fast they couldn't stop it.

"What made you go in that house anyway?"

Bennett shrugged.

"Our parents told us about this evil pumpkin who lived in this house. We thought they were just making it up to scare us, and we wanted to see if the stories were true."

"Yeah," Amy whispered, her face a mask of fear and angst.

"Maybe next time, take your parents' advice and stay out of dangerous situations. There's a reason why they're telling you to stay away from certain places," the officer advised.

"Yes, sir," they replied.

They watched the paramedics load Claudia's body into the back of the ambulance.

"Come on, kids," the police officer said. "Let's get you home."

As Amy and Bennett sat in the back of the police car for the ride home, both were lost in their own thoughts of the events of that night.

Never again would they test their parents' stories.

MORDECAI

In a mountain village nestled deep within the misty woods, a sinister presence lurked in the shadows. The townsfolk whispered of a vampire, a creature of the night, who thirsted for the blood of humans.

Mordecai had an insatiable hunger that could only be quenched by human blood.

Under the cloak of darkness, Mordecai would stealthily prowl through the streets, his eyes glowing with a sinister crimson hue. Searching for vulnerable souls, he was drawn to the innocence and purity that radiated from the village's young ones.

He watched quietly from the shadows as children walked along the dark village streets with their parents or friends, on their way home at the end of the day.

Mordecai preferred finding a child walking alone at night, but that was rare these days.

"Hey Darlene!" He heard a child yell. "Wanna come over to my house for a sleepover?"

"I can't," he heard a young girl reply, and assumed it was Darlene.

He turned his head toward the voice of Darlene and was mesmerized by her cherub appearance. Oh, how *delicious* must be her blood! He thought.

Darlene and the other girl parted ways when the other girl walked up the steps to her house and entered through the front door.

Mordecai began silently following Darlene, hoping to get a taste of that fresh, young blood before she got home; but Darlene entered the house just two doors down from the other girl.

This made things a bit more difficult for Mordecai, but not by much. He simply had to figure out which bedroom was hers and wait a while after the lights turned out to fulfil his insidious desires.

As she slept soundly in her bed, unaware of the impending danger, Mordecai slithered into her room, his fangs glistening with anticipation. His mouth filled with saliva at the promising taste of her sweet, young blood.

With a swift and silent movement, Mordecai hovered above Darlene, his cold breath caressing her delicate neck.

Just as he sank his fangs into her tender flesh, she woke up and let out a short, startled scream, which was quickly silenced as Mordecai drained the blood from her body, savoring every last drop.

He sat there for a while, reliving the experience in his mind over and over. Her blood was the best he'd tasted in a long time.

When he was satisfied, he silently transformed into a bat and flew out her open bedroom window.

Taking one last look at Darlene, Mordecai admired how calm she looked...as if she were sleeping peacefully.

The next morning, Darlene's mother was concerned when her daughter didn't come to breakfast and went to Darlene's room to check on her.

"Darlene, it's time to get up," she said firmly, assuming her daughter was being lazy and didn't want to go to school.

The silence in the room was deafening and gave Darlene's mother chills.

"Darlene?" She asked nervously as she walked closer to her daughter's bed.

She gasped when she saw how pale Darlene was in the morning light. Emily reached out and placed a hand on Darlene's forehead to check for a temperature.

She screamed when she felt her daughter's ice-cold forehead, knowing she was dead.

"Help! Help!" Emily screamed as loud as she could.

Frank, Darlene's father, came rushing into the room.

"What's wrong?" he asked in a panic.

"Darlene's dead!" Emily cried.

"What?!" Frank demanded, as he too ran over to Darlene's body and felt her forehead.

The icy feel of her flesh told him what he already knew, but he couldn't believe it. He placed two fingers on her neck to feel for a pulse. He felt nothing but icy cold skin and some odd bumps.

Frank pulled his fingers away and looked at them, noticing a dark smudge on his fingertips. He peered closely at Darlene's neck where he had placed his fingers and saw two, circular puncture wounds on her neck...right on her jugular vein.

Frank gasped and whispered in horror, *"Mordecai!"*

News of Darlene's murder spread through the village, striking fear into the hearts of parents. They knew they had to protect their children from this ancient evil. The townsfolk established a sundown curfew for every resident, so that nobody would be outside during the darkness of night.

Although this made some people feel a bit at ease, they couldn't help but remember that Darlene was in her own home in bed when she was murdered.

"How do we keep safe from Mordecai when we're *inside* our homes?" One fearful mother worried aloud at the next town meeting, which was held at night at the elementary school.

The audience was silent as people thought about ways to stay safe at home.

Suddenly, they heard an ethereal, girl's voice that seemed to come from every corner of the room.

"It's not Mordecai you need to worry about," the voice said with an evil laugh.

And then the lights went out, causing people to scream in fear. They ran to the exit doors to escape but couldn't open them. They simply wouldn't budge. The room instantly became engulfed in flames, burning everyone to ashes.

Mordecai and Darlene watched with glee as the building burnt and the people inside screamed in agony as the flames ate away at their flesh.

"Good job, Darlene," Mordecai smiled as they walked away from the destruction they caused.

GALIENA & HELEN

In the hamlet of Windsor were two witches who thrived on darkness and mischief. Galiena and Helen, devised a sinister plan to lure unsuspecting children into their clutches. They transformed themselves into innocent-looking children, their wicked intentions hidden beneath innocent smiles.

One moonlit evening, as the village children played in the park, Galiena and Helen approached with their deceitful charm.

"Hello!" Galiena greeted the children cheerfully.
She appeared as a little girl, the same age as the children playing.

"We're new in town. Would you like to play with us?"

"Sure!" A boy named Ian replied. "I'm Ian. What are your names?"

"I'm Jennifer, and this is my sister, Kristen," Helen said. "We live in the big house just beyond the woods."

The children stopped playing and looked at Jennifer and Kristen.

Paula, one of the little girls playing hopscotch, stopped and said fearfully, "The haunted house?"

Kristen laughed, "It's not haunted, silly!"

Mikey commented, "It *looks* haunted!"

"It just looks haunted because it's old," Jennifer replied with a giggle.

"She's right," Kristen agreed. "It's actually really beautiful inside and is filled with toys and treats. You should come over and play with us sometime."

"That sounds amazing!" Lily said, excitedly.

Lily had a big, sweet tooth, and would do anything to get candy.

"Let's go!" She urged.

Excitement filled the air as the children followed Jennifer and Kristen through the dark forest. The witches' house stood ominously, its windows adorned with eerie shadows.

"This place looks creepy," Mikey fretted. "Are you sure it's safe?"

Kristen laughed and said, "Of course! It's just an old house. Come inside, we have a surprise for you."

Although the children were a bit uneasy at the idea, their curiosity overcame them and they entered the witches' lair.

Quinn, the oldest of the children, mumbled to the others, "I don't like this, guys. Something doesn't feel right."

"Oh, don't be a stick in the mud, Quinn," Lily argued.

She was Quinn's little sister and was irritated with how he was always so cautious about everything. It tended to make life boring when he was around.

As they entered the house, the witches heard the children "oooh" and "aaah" and smiled at each other knowingly.

Inside, the house was adorned with enchanting decorations and shelves filled with curious objects. The children's eyes widened with wonder. Even Quinn was momentarily distracted from the danger lurking beneath the surface.

Nancy's eyes widened with wonder. She had never seen such a beautiful house.

"Wow, this place is amazing!" She squealed. "Where are the toys?"

Galiena waved her hand dismissively.

"Oh, they're hidden away in a secret room. But first, we must perform a special ritual to ensure our friendship."

Olive, always the suspicious child in the group, inquired, "What kind of ritual?"

"It's a game of trust," Helen began. "We blindfold each other and take turns guiding one another through the house. Don't worry, we'll keep you safe."

One by one, the children allowed themselves to be blindfolded, unaware of the witches' true intentions.

As the game commenced, the witches skillfully led the children through a labyrinth of hallways, their laughter echoing with malicious delight.

Paula whimpered, "This is getting scary. I want to go home."

"Don't be scared. Trust us a little longer," Jennifer said soothingly. "The surprise is just around the corner."

Minutes turned into hours, and the children's fear grew stronger, their pleas for release ignored by their captors.

Quinn was frustrated and said sternly, "*Enough! We want to leave now!*"

Kristen giggled and said, "Oh, you silly children. Did you really think we would let you go?"

Frightened by Kristen's comment, the children quickly removed their blindfolds and saw Galiena and Helen in their true forms, their faces contorted with wicked glee.

All the children screamed in terror!

"You see, children, we feed on your innocence and youth," Galiena explained. "Once we have drained you of your essence, you will become mere shadows of your former selves."

Reanna yelled, *"No! We won't let you!"*

With a surge of courage, the children banded together, using their wits and resourcefulness to escape the clutches of the witches.

They navigated the treacherous house, evading traps and overcoming obstacles until they reached the exit.

As they burst through the front door, the morning sun bathed their faces, and Shelly yelled, *"We're free! We made it!"*

"That's right!" Galiena laughed wickedly. "You made it!"

"All the way to our playroom," Helen said ominously.

The children stood there looking confused as the outdoors suddenly turned into a dark room filled with cauldrons, spell books, and tools used for torture.

"Noooo!" Quinn yelled.

Before the children could do anything to save themselves, they found themselves locked in a cell crawling with flea-ridden rats and spiders.

Galiena and Helen danced around the metal cell chanting words the children had never heard before. One by one, the children fell to the floor as the witches' powers withdrew the life-essence from each child, until they were all just a shell of their former selves.

Once their parents' noticed the children were missing, they spent months looking everywhere for them. Everywhere except for the witches' house in the dark woods...

DOPPELGANGER DANGER

In the lively, movie capital of the world, lived a young girl named Tammy. She was known for her kind heart and gentle nature, always ready to lend a helping hand to anyone in need. One fateful night, as the moon cast an eerie glow over Hollywood, an inexplicable incident occurred that would forever change Tammy's life.

She had just finished her evening routine and was about to brush her teeth before going to bed. As she stood in front of the bathroom mirror, she noticed something peculiar.

A flicker of movement caught her eye.

To her astonishment, she saw another version of herself staring back from within the mirror's depths.

Fear gripped Tammy's heart as she observed the reflection. The other Tammy had an eerie smile plastered on her face, her eyes filled with malice.

It didn't take long for Tammy to realize this other version of herself was not to be trusted. She watched in horror as the mirror-Tammy began to twist her once innocent existence into something dark and malevolent.

Tammy stared into the mirror and watched scenes played out by her doppelganger in what seemed like a movie.

A horror movie, that is.

In the reflection, Tammy's doppelganger started to perform wicked acts. She would hurt innocent animals, causing them pain and suffering.

Tammy reached out instinctively to try to save them but would be stopped by the hard surface of the mirror. When she did this, her doppelganger would let loose a wicked laugh.

Tammy's doppelganger would also manipulate people's minds, whispering words of malice and driving them to commit terrible deeds. The mirror-Tammy reveled in chaos and destruction, relishing the pain she caused...even to the real Tammy.

The most terrifying part was that the consequences of these acts became real in the physical world.

Tammy would wake up to find injured animals outside her doorstep. News reports would reveal people turning against each other in fits of rage and violence.

It seemed that the mirror-Tammy possessed an unholy power to make her evil intentions come to life.

Desperate to put an end to this nightmare, Tammy sought help from an old wise woman who lived in the San Fernando Valley. The wise woman listened intently to Tammy's tale, her face etched with concern.

"My dear child," the wise woman said, "You have encountered a malevolent spirit, a twisted reflection of your own soul. To banish this darkness, you must confront it with the purest form of love and compassion."

Armed with the wise woman's advice, Tammy returned home determined to face her mirror doppelganger.

As she stood before the mirror once again, the malevolent reflection grinned wickedly.

"You cannot defeat me," the mirror-Tammy sneered. "I am you, your darkest desires and impulses."

But Tammy remained resolute.

With every ounce of love and compassion she could muster, she reached out to the mirror-Tammy, enveloping her in a warm embrace.

As their bodies touched, a blinding light engulfed the room, and the mirror shattered into a thousand pieces.

When Tammy opened her eyes, she found herself alone in the bathroom, the shards of the broken mirror scattered on the floor. The malevolent reflection was gone, banished forever from her life, but its effects still remained.

Mirror-Tammy's manipulation and whispers of malice had a detrimental effect on those around Tammy.

The people in Tammy's life became increasingly suspicious and distrustful of each other, as the mirror-Tammy's influence seeped into their minds. Friends turned against each other, relationships crumbled, and families were torn apart by the toxic seeds of doubt and animosity planted by mirror-Tammy.

The once harmonious and supportive community became a breeding ground for anger, resentment, and conflict. The mirror-Tammy's wicked acts created a pervasive atmosphere of fear and paranoia, leaving a lasting impact on the emotional well-being and relationships of those affected.

The manipulation and whispers of malice instilled deep-seated feelings of distrust, betrayal, and fear within individuals. They were left questioning the authenticity of their relationships and doubting the intentions of their loved ones.

The toxic environment created by mirror-Tammy's actions left deep scars that were not easily healed.

Even after the influence of mirror-Tammy subsided, the lingering effects continued to haunt the affected individuals, making it challenging for them to trust and form meaningful connections again.

Overall, Mirror-Tammy's wicked acts left a lasting impact on the emotional well-being and relationships of those affected, forever altering their perception of trust and their ability to forge healthy connections with others.

ASTRAL PROJECTION

The wind howled outside, rattling the windows of Uma's small, cozy room. She sat cross-legged on her bed, listening intently to her friend, Valerie, as she spoke excitedly about astral projection. Valerie had always been intrigued by the mystical and unknown, and her latest fascination had captured Uma's curiosity.

"Imagine, Uma," Valerie said, her eyes sparkling with excitement. "Astral projection allows you to separate your consciousness from your physical body and explore the realms beyond. It's like traveling in a dream, but you're fully aware and in control."

Uma's heart raced with anticipation. The idea of exploring unseen dimensions and unlocking hidden secrets was both thrilling and terrifying. She had always been open-minded, but this was a whole new level of exploration.

"Can anyone do it?" Uma asked, her voice filled with a mix of excitement and apprehension.

Valerie nodded.

"Anyone with a strong enough will and focus can do it. It takes practice and concentration, but once you master it, the possibilities are endless."

With Valerie's guidance, Uma spent the next few days researching astral projection techniques. She meditated, practiced visualizations, and studied the experiences of others who had delved into this mystical practice.

Finally, feeling prepared, she decided to try it for herself.

That night, Uma lay in bed, her body relaxed, and her mind focused. She closed her eyes and began to visualize herself floating above her body. Gradually, she felt a strange sensation, as if her spirit was being gently pulled away from her physical form.

Moments later, Uma opened her eyes and found herself standing in her room, her body lying motionless on the bed. Excitement and awe filled her as she looked around. Everything appeared ethereal and slightly distorted.

As Uma floated through her house, she marveled at the freedom and weightlessness she felt. It was like she was a ghost, invisible and untethered. But as she tried to return to her body, a sudden sense of panic washed over her.

She rushed back to her room, only to find her physical body still lying on the bed, unmoving. Fear gripped her as she realized that she couldn't re-enter her own body. Someone, or something, had taken it over.

Desperation fueled her determination, and Uma began searching for answers. She floated through the walls of her house, passing through objects as if they were wisps of smoke. She soon discovered that she wasn't alone in this astral plane.

In the distance, she spotted a figure, shrouded in darkness.

As she approached, Uma could sense an eerie presence emanating from it. The figure turned towards her, revealing a sinister smile.

"You should have never meddled with forces you don't understand," the figure hissed, its voice sending chills down Uma's spine.

"Who are you? What have you done with my body?" Uma demanded, her voice filled with a mix of anger and fear.

The figure chuckled darkly.

"Your body is mine now. I have taken control. And you, my dear, are trapped in this astral realm forever."

Uma's heart pounded in her chest as she realized the gravity of the situation. She had unknowingly stumbled upon a malevolent entity that sought to steal her physical existence. Determined not to succumb, she mustered all her strength and confronted the figure head-on.

With every ounce of willpower, Uma fought to regain control over her own body. She visualized herself merging back into her physical form, refusing to let the darkness consume her. Slowly, she felt a powerful surge of energy coursing through her, and with a blinding flash, she was back.

Gasping for air, Uma found herself lying on her bed, drenched in sweat. Relief washed over her as she realized she had successfully returned to her body. She vowed never to dabble with astral projection again, knowing the dangers that lurked in the unknown.

From that day forward, Uma's life returned to normal, but the memory of that spine-tingling encounter haunted her. She had learned the hard way that some realms were best left unexplored, and the consequences of meddling with forces beyond comprehension could be truly terrifying.

THE SAINTLY WEREWOLF

In the middle-class town of Moorpark lived a humble and devout priest named Father Wesley. He was beloved by his parishioners for his kind heart, wise counsel, and unwavering faith. Little did he know that his life was about to take a dark and unexpected turn.

One fateful night, Father Wesley went for a walk and wandered through the hills after finishing his evening prayers. As he strolled beneath the pale moonlight, a rustling sound caught his attention.

Curiosity piqued, he followed the noise until he stumbled upon a wounded creature lying in the underbrush.

Filled with compassion, Father Wesley approached the creature to offer his aid. However, as he drew nearer, the injured creature revealed itself to be a powerful and fearsome werewolf.

In a flash, the creature lunged at him, sinking its teeth deep into Father Wesley's flesh. The pain was excruciating, and Father Wesley collapsed to the ground, barely conscious.

When he awoke, he found himself back in his humble abode, surrounded by the familiar sights and sounds of his church. Confused and disoriented, he tried to piece together the events of the previous night.

Days turned into weeks, and Father Wesley carried on with his duties as a priest, unaware of the curse that had befallen him. His encounters with the full moon were accompanied by strange dreams and unexplained restlessness, but he dismissed them as mere coincidences.

One fateful evening, Father Wesley was leading a midnight mass. The atmosphere in the church was serene, and his voice filled the air with the soothing melodies of prayer. As he reached the climax of the service, the full moon emerged from behind a dark cloud, casting an eerie glow through the stained-glass windows.

Suddenly, an intense pain coursed through Father Wesley's body, causing him to stumble mid-sentence. He clutched his chest, feeling his bones shift and reshape. In a matter of seconds, his human form was replaced by the terrifying visage of a werewolf.

As the congregation gasped in horror, Father Wesley's newfound instincts took over, and he leaped from the pulpit, his eyes glowing with a primal hunger. Chaos ensued as he pounced on unsuspecting parishioners, tearing through the pews with savage fury.

The once peaceful church became a scene of terror and bloodshed. Father Wesley, now consumed by his monstrous nature, lost all control over his actions. The people who had once sought solace in his guidance were now victims of his insatiable hunger.

Outside the church, the townsfolk, alerted by the screams, gathered in an attempt to understand the horrifying events unfolding within. As they cautiously approached the entrance, they were met with the chilling sight of their beloved priest, transformed into a nightmarish creature.

In a desperate effort to protect themselves and their community, the townsfolk armed themselves with makeshift weapons and prepared to confront the werewolf. It was a battle of survival, a fight against the darkness that had consumed their once-devoted spiritual leader.

The clash between the townsfolk and the werewolf raged on, with neither side willing to yield.

Finally, as the first rays of dawn began to break through the horizon, weakening the werewolf's powers, the townsfolk managed to subdue Father Wesley.

As the sun's rays touched his fur-covered skin, Father Wesley reverted to his human form, naked and covered in blood. Confusion and guilt washed over him as he looked upon the devastation he had caused. The realization of his transformation and the horrors he had committed dawned upon him.

In the aftermath of the tragic night, the townsfolk, though shaken to their core, forgave Father Wesley for the horrors he had inflicted upon them. They understood that he had become a victim of a curse beyond his control.

Father Wesley, burdened with guilt and remorse, dedicated the rest of his life to seeking redemption. He withdrew from the world, devoting himself to understanding and suppressing the curse within him.

Through his unwavering faith and tireless efforts, he found solace and a way to control his inner beast.

His tale became a cautionary legend, a reminder that even the most devout and virtuous among us can fall victim to the darkness that lurks within. And so, the town mourned the loss of their innocence, forever haunted by the memory of that dreadful night when their priest became a nightmare.

CASINO PONTIANAK

Once a year, the bustling city of Las Vegas would transform into a hub of excitement and adrenaline as the annual race took place. People from far and wide gathered to witness the thrilling spectacle, with engines roaring and tires screeching through the neon-lit streets.

However, little did they know that amidst the cheers and applause, an ancient terror lurked in the shadows, waiting to unleash its malevolence upon the city.

Legend had it that a Pontianak, a vengeful female spirit from Southeast Asian folklore, had been awakened by the chaos and energy of the race. Drawn to the vibrant energy of Las

Vegas, she sought to wreak havoc and sow fear among the unsuspecting participants and spectators.

As the sun set on the day of the race, a sense of unease settled over the city.

Xiao, a little girl who was sitting in the bleachers with her parents, waiting for the race to begin, felt an icy chill envelop the air around her. She shivered and pulled her jacket tighter around her small frame as she looked around for the cause of the sudden cold.

Not seeing anything near her, she looked up to the sky and noticed that dark clouds veiled the moon, casting an eerie glow over the Las Vegas Strip.

The sound of screeching tires was soon drowned out by the haunting whispers of a baby crying, carried by the desert wind for all to hear.

The Pontianak had arrived.

Her presence was felt before she was seen, a chill that sent shivers down the spines of anyone in her proximity.

The Pontianak's ethereal figure emerged from the shadows, her long, flowing hair obscuring her pale face. Having died while giving birth, she was dressed in a torn and bloodstained white gown. She glided silently through the neon-lit streets, her eyes glowing with a sinister intensity.

As the race progressed, chaos ensued. The Pontianak targeted the race participants, appearing suddenly in front of speeding cars, causing drivers to lose control and crash in a flurry of twisted metal and shattered glass. Once their cars came to a stop, the Pontianak glided over to them, dug her razor-sharp nails into their abdomens and devoured their organs while the drivers were still barely alive.

Panic spread like wildfire among the spectators as they witnessed the horrifying attacks. The once jubilant atmosphere turned into a nightmare.

No one was safe from the Pontianak's wrath.

She materialized in rearview mirrors, her blood-red eyes reflecting the terror of her victims before she lunged at them with supernatural strength and ferocity.

Her wails echoed through the city, a haunting melody that struck fear into the hearts of all who heard it.

The authorities were baffled and helpless in the face of this supernatural menace. The Pontianak seemed unstoppable, her power growing with each passing moment. Fear gripped the city, and the annual race became synonymous with death and terror.

But amidst the darkness, a glimmer of hope emerged. A group of brave individuals, determined to end the Pontianak's reign of terror, banded together. Armed with ancient rituals and talismans, they sought to confront the vengeful spirit and put an end to her rampage.

In a final showdown, the group lured the Pontianak to an abandoned racetrack on the outskirts of the city. They chanted incantations and brandished sacred relics, their faith and determination fueling their courage. As the Pontianak descended upon them, they unleashed their collective power, binding her spirit and sealing her away.

With the Pontianak banished, the city of Las Vegas slowly regained its composure. The annual race, once tainted by fear, returned to its former glory.

But the memory of that fateful night lingered, a reminder of the darkness that had gripped the city. And every year, as the race commenced, a silent prayer was whispered, hoping that the Pontianak would never return to haunt the streets of Las Vegas again.

MIDNIGHT LIBRARY

There once was a library that nobody visited after dark. It stood at the end of Willow Street, its tall, ancient windows looking out like sleepy eyes. By day, children loved to visit, to read stories, and borrow books. But at night, the library's doors creaked shut, and the lights dimmed, casting long, eerie shadows.

There was a rumor among the children that after the clock struck twelve, the books inside the library woke up.

One chilly October evening, three friends—Yasmin, Zachary, and Max—decided to investigate. They'd heard whispers about the

"Midnight Library" but didn't believe the tales of ghostly stories and vanishing books.

Armed with nothing but a flashlight and their courage, they sneaked out of their homes and tiptoed down Willow Street.

As they reached the grand library doors, they hesitated. What if the rumors were true?

Max, the bravest of them, pushed open the doors with a loud creak. Inside, everything looked normal—rows and rows of bookshelves, the soft rustle of pages in the breeze from a slightly open window, and a large grandfather clock ticking away in the corner. They wandered around, feeling both nervous and excited.

But then, something strange happened. The clock struck twelve.

DONG…DONG…DONG...DONG...DONG...DONG...DONG...DONG...DONG...DONG... DONG...DONG

Suddenly, the library seemed to come alive! Books began to slide off the shelves on their own, thudding onto the floor. Shadows stretched and twisted unnaturally, and faint whispers filled the air. Zachary's eyes widened as a storybook floated off a shelf and hovered in front of them.

"Did you see that?" whispered Yasmin, gripping Max's arm.

The book flipped open, and the pages began to turn, faster and faster. Words leapt off the paper and floated around them like mist. Then, from between the lines of the story, a pale, ghostly figure emerged.

She was a girl, dressed in a long, flowing dress, her eyes glowing faintly in the dark.

"Who are you?" asked Max, his voice shaking.

The ghost smiled, but there was something sad in her expression.

"I am Elizabeth," she whispered. "Long ago, I was like you—a child who loved stories. But one night, I stayed too late, and now I am bound to the Midnight Library."

Yasmin, Zachary, and Max stepped back, eyes wide with fear. They could hear more pages rustling, more voices whispering from the books around them.

Elizabeth looked at them pleadingly.

"I can't leave until someone reads my story. Will you help me?"

The friends exchanged nervous glances. They didn't want to upset the ghost, but they also weren't sure they could trust her.

Zachary, the kindest of them all, nodded.

"We'll help," he said softly.

The book that had brought Elizabeth to life floated down to Zachary's hands. He opened it and began to read aloud, his voice trembling slightly.

"Once there was a little girl named Elizabeth who loved books more than anything..."

As Zachary read, the library grew quieter. The whispering stopped, and the shadows shrank back into their places. Elizabeth listened with a peaceful smile, and as the story came to an end, her form began to fade.

"Thank you," she whispered, her voice barely audible. "Now, I can rest..."

With that, Elizabeth disappeared, leaving only the faint scent of old paper and a feeling of calm.

The friends stood there for a moment, staring at the spot where she had been. Then, without a word, they quietly closed the book and placed it back on the shelf.

As they turned to leave, the library seemed to sigh in relief, and the grandfather clock ticked softly once more.

They hurried out into the night, feeling both spooked and relieved.

From that night on, the Midnight Library stayed quiet. And though they never spoke of it again, the friends would always remember the ghostly girl who had been waiting for someone to read her story.

NIGHT OF THE WALKING DEAD

When the leaves on the trees turn to shades of yellow, orange and read, everyone in Godric's Hollow knew to be indoors before sunset...especially in October.

It was said that when the last rays of sunlight disappeared behind the hills, the ground in the old graveyard started to stir.

People whispered about the walking dead— zombies who woke from their slumber and wandered the streets, looking for anyone who dared to stay out after dark.

But Timmy, who had just moved to Godric's Hollow, didn't believe in such things.

"Zombies aren't real," he laughed as he played outside with his dog, Bentley, one cool autumn evening.

"Timmy, come inside before it gets dark!" his mum called from the porch, but Timmy ignored her, determined to kick his football just one more time.

As the sky turned purple and the sun dipped behind the hills, Bentley suddenly stopped chasing the ball and began to growl softly.

Timmy froze, his smile fading. He hadn't realized how quiet the street had become. The air felt heavy, and a strange mist began to rise from the ground.

In the distance, a low, eerie moaning sound echoed. Timmy's heart raced. He grabbed Bentley's leash and hurried toward the house, but before he could make it, he saw something moving at the far end of the street.

A figure stumbled into view, dragging its feet across the ground. Its clothes were old and torn, and its skin was a sickly gray. Its eyes, dull and lifeless, stared straight ahead.

Timmy gulped and took a step back, but the zombie wasn't alone. More shapes were emerging from the shadows—slow, shuffling figures with outstretched arms, their eyes glowing faintly in the dark.

Bentley barked and tugged on the leash, but Timmy was frozen in place, staring at the approaching horde. They were coming closer, their raspy breaths and slow, dragging steps filling the air.

"I have to get inside," Timmy whispered to himself, trying to calm his racing heart.

Gathering all his courage, Timmy turned and bolted toward his house, Bentley right behind him. But as he ran, he glanced over his shoulder and saw more zombies—climbing over fences, stumbling out of alleyways, all heading toward him.

He reached his front door and pounded on it, shouting, "Mum! Mum, open up!"

The door flew open, and Timmy scrambled inside just as the first zombie reached the porch. His mum slammed the door shut, bolting it tightly.

"I told you to come in before dark!" she scolded, her face pale with fear.

But Timmy could tell she was just as scared as he was.

From the window, they watched the zombies shuffle by, their shadowy forms stumbling through the mist. Timmy's heart pounded as he realized just how close he had come to being caught by the walking dead.

Suddenly, Bentley started barking again. Timmy glanced out the window and saw something even scarier—a small figure moving through the street. It was Timmy's neighbor, Clarice. She had forgotten to go inside, too!

Timmy's mum gasped. "We have to help her!"

Timmy didn't need to be told twice. He grabbed his flashlight, the one with the super bright beam, and ran to the back door.

"Wait!" his mum called, but Timmy was already out the door, Bentley by his side.

He sprinted toward Clarice, shining his flashlight at the zombies.

The beam of light seemed to confuse them, and they stopped in their tracks, turning away from the brightness.

Timmy reached Clarice just as a zombie reached out a bony hand toward her. He flashed the light right in its face, and the zombie recoiled, stumbling back into the mist.

"Come on!" Timmy shouted, grabbing Clarice's hand.

Together, they ran back to Timmy's house, shining the flashlight at any zombie that came too close. The zombies seemed afraid of the light, moving sluggishly and groaning as they shied away from the beam.

They made it inside just as the mist thickened, and Timmy's mum slammed the door shut behind them once again. Bentley barked a warning, but the zombies didn't try to break in. Instead, they wandered the streets, looking for anyone left outside.

Timmy and Clarice peeked out the window, watching as the zombies slowly faded back into the shadows, disappearing one by one. By morning, they would be gone, buried once more in the graveyard where they belonged.

That night, as Timmy lay in bed, he thought about how close he had come to being caught by the zombies. From that day on, he made sure to be inside well before dark. Because in Godric's Hollow, when the sun goes down, the zombies rise—and they never stop looking for someone to join them.

BRIDGE OF THE DARK FOREST

Once upon a time, in a village at the edge of the Dark Forest, there was a legend about a bridge deep within the woods. The bridge was old and crumbling, its stones covered in moss and vines. It wasn't just any ordinary bridge. Rumor had it that a troll lived beneath it, and anyone who crossed after sunset would never return.

Most children in the village knew to stay far away from the bridge. But Lorenzo, didn't believe in trolls or any of the spooky stories the grown-ups told.

He rolled his eyes whenever the other kids talked about the legend. "It's just a scary story to keep us out of the woods."

One autumn evening, Lorenzo's curiosity got the best of him. He decided to prove once and for all that the legend was nonsense.

He grabbed his lantern and ventured into the Dark Forest. The trees were tall and twisted, their branches forming strange shapes in the fading light. The deeper Lorenzo went, the quieter the forest became. No birds chirped, no crickets sang. Only the sound of his footsteps crunching on the dead leaves at his feet echoed through the woods.

After what seemed like hours of walking, Lorenzo finally came upon the old bridge. It looked just as the stories said—crumbling, ancient, and forgotten. The stream below was barely more than a trickle, and the wind whistled through the gaps in the stones.

Lorenzo took a deep breath.

"See? No trolls," he muttered, stepping onto the bridge.

But just as his foot touched the first stone, a deep, rumbling voice came from beneath.

"Who dares to cross my bridge?!"

Lorenzo froze, his heart pounding so hard it made his shirt move with it.

The voice was low and gravelly, as if it came from the very earth itself.

"I—I didn't know anyone lived here," Lorenzo stammered, gripping his lantern tightly.

From under the bridge, a large, shadowy figure began to emerge.

It was as tall as two men, with thick, warty skin and glowing yellow eyes that glared at Lorenzo. Its arms were long and powerful, and its teeth, sharp as broken stones, gleamed in the dim light.

"You have disturbed my slumber, little human," growled the troll, his voice like the sound of rocks grinding together. "No one crosses my bridge without a price."

Lorenzo's legs trembled, but he didn't run.

He had always thought the stories were just tales, but now, faced with the enormous troll, he realized he was wrong.

"Wh-what do you want?" Lorenzo asked, his voice shaking.

The troll grinned, revealing rows of jagged teeth.

"A riddle," he said. "If you answer correctly, I will let you pass. But if you fail... well, I will have myself a little snack."

Lorenzo's heart sank.

He was terrible at riddles. But there was no way back—he had to try.

The troll leaned in closer, his foul breath filling the air.

"Here is my riddle," the troll rumbled. "I have no eyes, but once I did see. I used to have thoughts, but now I am empty. What am I?"

Lorenzo's mind raced. He thought about the troll's words. No eyes, but once could see? Used to have thoughts, but now empty?

The troll's yellow eyes gleamed as it waited for an answer.

Suddenly, Lorenzo remembered something his grandmother once said about the forest—that sometimes, you can find clues in nature. His gaze fell to the ground, and there, near the edge of the bridge, was an old skull, half-buried in the dirt.

"A skull!" Lorenzo blurted out. "The answer is a skull!"

The troll's eyes widened, and for a moment, Lorenzo thought it might attack anyway. But then the troll threw back its head and let out a deep, rumbling laugh that shook the stones of the bridge.

"Clever boy," the troll said, stepping back into the shadows. "You have answered correctly. You may pass."

Lorenzo didn't need to be told twice. He ran across the bridge, his heart pounding with every step. The moment he reached the other side, he glanced back. The troll had disappeared beneath the bridge once more, melting into the shadows.

Lorenzo hurried home, vowing never to venture into the Dark Forest again. From that day on, he warned the other children not to go near the bridge at night. But some nights, when the wind howled through the village, Lorenzo could swear he heard the troll's deep voice in the distance, rumbling beneath the stones.

And he knew that the troll would always be there, waiting for the next traveler who dared to cross the bridge of the dark forest.

MYSTERY OF THE CHUPACABRA

In a small, Mexican village nestled between the hills and the forest, strange things had been happening. Animals began disappearing from their pens at night—goats, chickens, even a few dogs. All the villagers were talking about it, but no one knew what was behind the mysterious disappearances.

Except for one thing... every morning, the animals' pens were left with strange, small holes in the ground, and tiny spots of blood near them.

Some whispered about the legend of the Chupacabra—a creature that was said to roam the forests, sucking the blood from livestock.

No one had ever seen it, but everyone feared it.

Juanita, a 10-year-old girl, lived on the edge of the village with her parents and younger brother. They had a small farm with goats, and one evening, her father came in looking worried.

"Another goat is missing," he said. "We have to be more careful. They say it could be the Chupacabra."

Juanita had heard the stories, and a chill ran down her spine.

"How can we be more careful, Papa?" she asked.

Her father just sighed. "Be sure to lock up the animals tight tonight."

"Okay," she said, but wasn't sure how she could lock them up more tightly than she always did.

Having always heard the stories about the frightening chupacabra, she had never actually seen one, or even heard what they looked like.

Juanita was curious. She wanted to find out more about it.

That night, after everyone had gone to bed, she snuck outside. The full moon bathed the farm in a silver glow, casting long shadows across the yard. Juanita quietly made her way to the goat pen, her heart pounding in her chest.

As she crouched down by the fence, a soft rustling sound caught her attention. She flicked on her flashlight and swept the beam across the field. There was nothing but tall grass swaying in the wind.

But then, her light caught something—two glowing red eyes staring at her from the edge of the forest.

Juanita froze, her hand trembling as she held the flashlight. The creature stepped forward, just enough for her to see it clearly. It was small, but its skin was dark and leathery, covered in patches of bristly hair. It walked on two legs, but hunched over like a wild animal, and its claws gleamed in the moonlight. Its mouth was filled with sharp, pointed teeth, and its eyes glowed like embers.

Juanita gasped and stumbled back, but the creature didn't move. It just stood there, watching her with its unblinking eyes.

Then, with a sudden, eerie hiss, it bolted toward the goat pen, moving faster than Juanita could believe.

"Stop!" Juanita shouted, her voice breaking the silence of the night.

Without thinking, she grabbed a stick from the ground and ran after it. The Chupacabra was already in the pen, its claws tearing at the wooden fence as the goats bleated in panic.

Juanita's heart pounded, but she didn't run away. Instead, she charged toward the creature, waving her flashlight and shouting as loud as she could. *"Get away from them!"*

The Chupacabra turned its head toward her, its glowing eyes narrowing. It hissed again and leaped toward Juanita, knocking her down before she could even realize what was happening.

It tore into her flesh with all four paws, sucking the blood from her wounds as soon as it appeared.

Within seconds, Juanita's shredded and lifeless body was discarded by the Chupacabra as it took its time feasting on the family's goats.

The next morning, when her parents found her body alongside the dead goats, they cried aloud and moaned in agony at their loss.

Noticing the flashlight lying on the ground near Juanita bloody body, it's light still illuminating the goats' pen, her father sobbed and said, "Juanita, what did you do? What has happened to my baby?"

"She didn't think it was real," her brother Julio mumbled. "She wanted to prove us wrong."

Her father frowned. "*Why?*"

Julio just shook his head and placed his arms around his mother's shoulders, which were heaving from her heartbroken sobs.

From then on, the villagers worked together to protect their animals, building stronger pens and keeping watch at night. They knew the

Chupacabra was still out there, somewhere in the forest, watching and waiting.

CRY OF THE BANSHEE

In Portmagee, a small Irish seaside village, there is a legend about the Banshee. Villagers spoke in whispers about the ghostly woman who appeared on stormy nights, her wailing cry heard on the wind.

They say that when you hear the Banshee's cry, it means someone is about to die.

Ten-year-old Fiona had heard the stories her whole life. She never believed them, thinking they were simply old wives' tales; but, always enjoyed hearing scary stories from her beloved grandmother.

Her younger brother, Colin, was always frightened by the Banshee stories, but Fiona would laugh at his fear.

One chilly autumn evening, a fierce storm rolled in. Wind howled through the trees, and rain lashed against the windows of their small cottage. Fiona and Colin sat by the fire, listening to the wind howl like a wild animal.

Suddenly, the wind seemed to change.

Instead of the usual whistling and gusts, they heard something else—something that sent a chill down Fiona's spine.

It was a long, high-pitched wail, rising and falling like a sad, mournful song.

Colin's eyes went wide, and he clutched his blanket tightly.

"Fiona," he whispered, "do you hear that?"

Fiona nodded, her heart pounding.

She didn't want to admit it, but the sound frightened her too. It wasn't like the wind or the rain.

It was a cry. A ghostly wail that seemed to echo from the hills beyond the village.

Their grandmother, who was sitting in her rocking chair by the fire, suddenly stood up, her face pale.

"That's the Banshee," she whispered. "I heard it before, long ago."

Fiona's stomach twisted in fear, but she forced a smile.

"It's just the wind, Grammy," she calmly assured her elderly grandmother.

But her grandmother shook her head, her eyes serious.

"I've lived many years, child. That is no wind. The Banshee is crying, and it means one thing—someone in this village will not live to see the morning."

Colin whimpered, and Fiona tried to comfort him, though she was trembling inside.

The wailing continued, growing louder and more haunting with every gust of wind.

Fiona could almost feel the sadness in it, like someone was grieving right outside their door.

"I'll prove it's just the wind," Fiona said suddenly, trying to sound brave.

She grabbed her coat and lantern, determined to show her family there was no ghostly woman out there.

"I'll be back soon."

"Fiona, no!" her grandmother cried, but Fiona was already at the door.

She stepped out into the storm, the rain stinging her face as the wind howled around her. The wail echoed through the night, making her shiver. Fiona held her lantern high and marched toward the hills, determined to find the source of the sound.

As she neared the edge of the village, she saw something that made her stop in her tracks.

Standing at the top of a hill, silhouetted against the stormy sky, was a figure. It was a woman, dressed in a tattered white gown, her long, pale hair blowing wildly in the wind. She was hunched over, her face hidden by her hair, but

Fiona could hear her crying—soft, mournful sobs that sent chills through her bones.

Fiona wanted to turn and run, but her feet wouldn't move. She stood frozen, staring at the ghostly figure. The Banshee's cries grew louder, more heart-wrenching, as if she were weeping for someone she loved.

Suddenly, the Banshee lifted her head, and though her face was hidden in shadow, Fiona could feel its eyes on her.

The Banshee pointed a long, bony finger toward the village, and Fiona understood. The Banshee wasn't just crying for someone—she was warning them.

Heart pounding, Fiona turned and ran as fast as she could back to the cottage. She burst through the door, soaking wet and out of breath.

"Grammy! Colin! We need to warn the village!"

Her grandmother nodded sadly, as if she already knew.

"It's too late, Fiona. The Banshee's cry is a warning, but it can't be stopped."

The storm raged through the night, and the next morning, the village woke to sad news. Old Mr. O'Malley, who lived on the far side of the village, had passed away in his sleep.

Fiona never doubted the legend of the Banshee again. From that night on, whenever the wind howled through the hills, she listened carefully, hoping never to hear that mournful wail again. Because now she knew the truth. The Banshee's cry was real, and it was a sound that no one ever wanted to hear.

GHOULS OF HOLLOW HAVEN

In a quiet village near the edge of a dark, twisted forest, there was an old, abandoned graveyard known as Hollow Hill. No one visited it anymore, not even during the day. It was overgrown with tangled vines, broken gravestones, and eerie silence. The villagers warned their children to never go near it, especially after sunset, because that's when the ghouls were said to come out.

The ghouls were once people, according to the legend—people who had grown greedy and wicked in life. Now they lived beneath the earth, feasting on bones and creeping out of their graves to steal away anyone foolish enough to wander nearby.

Twelve-year-old Sam didn't believe in ghouls. He thought it was just a story to scare kids and keep them from playing in the spooky graveyard.

"They're not real," Sam told his best friend, Jake, as they walked home from school one afternoon. "It's just a bunch of old graves."

"I wouldn't go there if I were you," Jake said, glancing nervously toward the dark forest in the distance. "My uncle said he saw something moving in the shadows near Hollow Hill once."

But Sam was a foolish boy who was determined to prove it was all just stories.

That evening, when the sky was turning orange and the shadows were growing long, he snuck out of the house and headed straight for Hollow Hill, determined to see the place for himself.

When Sam arrived at the graveyard, it was eerier than he expected. The sun had almost set, and the crooked gravestones cast long, dark shadows across the ground. The air felt cold and heavy, and the only sound was the rustling of the wind through the dead trees.

Sam shivered, but he wasn't about to turn back now.

He climbed over the rusty gate and made his way through the graveyard, stepping carefully over the broken stones and overgrown vines. His flashlight beam cut through the dim light, but everything seemed still and silent.

"See?" Sam whispered to himself. "No ghouls. Just old stones."

But just as he was about to turn back, he heard something. A faint scratching sound, like nails scraping against stone.

Sam froze, his heart pounding. The sound grew louder, coming from one of the graves nearby. He slowly turned his flashlight toward it.

The beam of light flickered across a large, cracked gravestone, and then—movement.

The ground beside the grave was shifting, as if something underneath was pushing up.

Sam's breath caught in his throat as a bony hand, pale and clawed, burst through the soil.

Sam screamed in spite of himself and watched as the horror unfolded around him.

The creature pulled itself out of the ground, its gray, shriveled skin clinging to its bones. Its eyes were dark, empty pits, and its mouth was full of sharp, jagged teeth.

It hissed softly, the sound like dried leaves scraping together, and then more hands began to claw their way out of the earth around it.

Sam backed away, his flashlight trembling in his hand. There were more ghouls, crawling up from their graves, their long fingers dragging across the ground as they rose.

They moved slowly at first, but then their heads snapped toward Sam, and they began to crawl and shuffle toward him, their bony hands reaching out.

Sam turned and ran, his heart pounding in his chest. The ghouls moved faster than he expected, their twisted bodies jerking forward as they chased after him. He could hear their hissing breaths and the scrape of their nails on the ground.

He reached the rusty gate and scrambled over it, not daring to look back. The ghouls' whispers filled the air behind him, growing fainter as he ran toward the village, faster than he'd ever run in his life.

When Sam finally burst through the door of his house, he was out of breath, his face pale.

His parents looked at him in surprise, but Sam didn't say a word. He knew no one would believe him.

From that night on, Sam never went near Hollow Hill again. And every time he walked past the edge of the forest, he felt the cold, hollow eyes of the ghouls watching him from the shadows, waiting for their next chance to crawl out of the earth.

The villagers still warned their children to stay away from Hollow Hill, but Sam didn't need any more warnings. He knew the truth now— that the ghouls were real, and they were always hungry.

ABOUT THE AUTHOR

LEANNE STABACK
(HALLOWEEN 2024)

Leanne Staback, Ph.D. was a teacher for many years and ran a successful, private tutoring company until she retired from teaching in 2020. Several of Dr. Staback's colleagues, familiar with her penchant for storytelling to make learning fun, encouraged her to begin writing children's stories. She wrote her first children's story "Christopher and the Bouncing Beagle", which turned out to be a best seller. This encouragement prompted Dr. Staback to continue writing children's stories both for educational purposes, and for fun! Dr. Staback is a Lady of the Scottish realm, married to Lord Rudy Hayes – a well-known singer in Las Vegas, has five children, and continues to write and work with illustrators to make her visions come to life for her young readers.

OTHER BOOKS BY LEANNE STABACK

Books for infants and toddlers
(Ages 0 – 3)

<u>Developing Baby's First 100 Words Series</u>
(Also coming in 2025 in Spanish and Tagalog!)

- Baby, Let's Talk! Book 1 – Social Words

- Baby, Let's Talk! Book 2 – Pronouns, Names and Location Words

- Baby, Let's Talk! Book 3 – Numbers and Quantity Words

- Baby, Let's Talk! Book 4 – Colors, Shapes, and Other Descriptive Words

- Baby, Let's Talk! Book 5 – Body Part Words

Books for children
(All ages)

- Christopher and the Bouncing Beagle

- Jaziel is a Big Brother!

- Kent and Leanne's Backyard Magic Show

- Little Nurse Lauretta

- Marc the Viking and the Wily Wolf (with Allyson Giolas)

- María and the Magic of Guanajuato

- Shawn and the Lion's Roar [textbook] (with Allyson Giolas)

- Shawn and the Lion's Roar Storybook (with Allyson Giolas)

- Sloane the Smiling Sloth [textbook] (with Allyson Giolas)

- Sloane the Smiling Sloth Storybook (with Allyson Giolas)

- The Brave Little Dreamer

Young Adult
(Age 13 – 18)

- 13 Terrifying Short Stories for Halloween

STILL TO COME IN 2024

Children's Books

- Around the World with St. Nicholas and Friends: Around the World Series, Vol. 1 (with Marlin Montgomery)

- Steven the Sea Turtle's Big Adventure [textbook] (with Allyson Giolas)

- Steven the Sea Turtle's Big Adventure Storybook with Allyson Giolas

STILL TO COME IN 2024

Young Adult Books

Andarta, Vol. 1: Legends Never Die, Prologue Promo Graphic Novelette (with Sloane Kennedy and Steve Bentley)

Andarta, Vol. 1: Legends Never Die (with Sloane Kennedy)